KIDNAPPED AT THE CAPITAL

by **Ron Roy**

illustrated by **Liza Woodruff**

A STEPPING STONE BOOK™

Random House New York

This book is for my parents, Marie and Zeke, who gave me my first book.
—R.R.

Text copyright © 2002 by Ron Roy
Interior illustrations copyright © 2002 by Liza Woodruff
Cover illustration copyright © 2010 by Greg Swearingen
Map copyright © 2003 by Timothy Bush

Visit us on the Web!
SteppingStonesBooks.com
www.randomhouse.com/kids

Educators and librarians, for a variety of teaching tools, visit us at
www.randomhouse.com/teachers

Library of Congress Cataloging-in-Publication Data
Roy, Ron.
Kidnapped at the Capital / by Ron Roy ; illustrated by Liza Woodruff.
    p. cm. — (Capital mysteries ; #2)
"A Stepping Stone Book."
Summary: KC's mother and the clone of the President of the United States are kidnapped by disgruntled astronauts who want to take over the International Space Station.
ISBN 978-0-307-26514-2 (pbk.) — ISBN 978-0-307-46514-6 (lib. bdg.)
[1. Kidnapping—Fiction. 2. Cloning—Fiction.] I. Woodruff, Liza, ill.
II. Title. III. Series.
PZ7.R8139 Ki 2003 [Fic]—dc21 2002156154

Printed in the United States of America
18 17

Contents

1. Vanished   1

2. Top Secret   10

3. Kidnapped   19

4. The Search Begins   27

5. Space Mission   35

6. Flowers on the Moon   42

7. Run and Hide   49

8. Doomed   58

9. 1600 Pennsylvania Avenue   65

1
Vanished

"Come and eat, kitties!" KC Corcoran called out. She filled a bowl with cat food and set it on the floor. Lost and Found, her two kittens, came sliding around the corner when they heard the sound.

Marshall Li, KC's best friend, poured water into another bowl.

"We have to leave soon," KC's mom said. Lois Corcoran held up an engraved invitation. "It's almost ten o'clock. The president is meeting us outside the Air and Space Museum in half an hour."

"Do you think Casey Marshall will be there, too?" KC asked.

"I doubt it," her mother said, looking for her keys. "The president doesn't want the public to know he has a clone."

The President of the United States had invited KC, her mom, and Marshall to the Cherry Blossom Festival. Each April, this celebration was held on the National Mall in Washington, D.C. Thousands of people came out to enjoy the museums and the beautiful pink cherry blossoms.

KC and Marshall had become friends with President Zachary Thornton when they'd rescued him from evil scientists. The scientists had cloned the president, hoping to use the clone for their own purposes.

But KC and Marshall had saved the president, and the president had saved the clone. Now the clone—named Casey

Marshall after KC and Marshall—lived in the White House.

"Do I have time to run downstairs and feed Spike?" Marshall asked.

Marshall lived in an apartment two floors below KC. He was staying with the Corcorans while his parents were away buying antiques for his mom's shop.

"If you hurry," KC's mom said. "We'll meet you in the lobby in five minutes."

KC watched Marshall dash out the door. Spike was his pet tarantula. KC shuddered, thinking of all those hairy legs.

Five minutes later, KC, her mom, and Marshall met in the lobby.

"Say hi to the president for me," said Donald. He held the door open. Donald was the building manager, and he was also their friend.

The National Mall was a short walk from the apartments. They passed the Capitol building, then cut through the Botanic Gardens. The cherry trees that lined the grassy strip were in full bloom. Everywhere KC looked, people were going in and out of the museums and other buildings on the National Mall.

Kids zoomed around on roller blades. Joggers dodged baby strollers. Vendors stood behind carts selling food, T-shirts, and Washington, D.C. souvenirs.

"There he is!" Marshall pointed to a group of people next to the National Air and Space Museum. In the center of the group stood the president, wearing khaki pants, a blue sweater, and a baseball cap. All around him were secret service agents in dark suits. The president chatted and shook hands with everyone who came up to him.

"Isn't it great," KC's mom said, "that President Thornton gets out to meet the people who elected him?"

The president looked up and waved at KC, her mom, and Marshall. The secret service agents made an opening for them through the crowd.

"Hi! Thanks for coming," the president said when they reached him. "Aren't the cherry blossoms beautiful?"

"Lovely!" KC's mom said. She picked a blossom from a tree and tucked it in her hair. "Thank you for inviting us, Mr. President."

"The cherry trees are so pink!" KC said. "I feel like I'm walking through strawberry ice cream!"

"Mmmm, ice cream!" said Marshall.

"Now there's a good idea," KC's mom said. "Would you like to get some?" She dug in her purse, then handed KC a five-dollar bill.

KC and Marshall went looking for an ice cream cart. "President Thornton is so cool," Marshall said. "Maybe I'll run for president some day."

"I thought you wanted to be a bug scientist," KC reminded her friend.

Marshall shrugged. "I can always be an entomologist in my spare time."

"I don't think presidents get much time for hobbies," KC said.

"That's lousy," Marshall said. "If I can't bring my spiders, I'm not gonna be president!"

KC laughed. "I'd vote for you, but only

6

if you made me the TV anchor for the White House."

Marshall spotted a group of food carts in front of the Smithsonian castle. He and KC walked over to a teenager selling ice cream cones.

"What'll it be?" the teenager asked.

"A cherry and pistachio cone, please," Marshall told the kid. "One scoop of each, with the pistachio on top."

"Awesome," the teenager said. "Looks like Christmas."

"I'll have butter crunch," KC said. "One scoop."

She paid with her mom's money, then they began walking back toward the Air and Space Museum.

"I wonder who planted all these cherry trees," Marshall said.

"Johnny Cherryseed," KC said, licking her cone.

Marshall laughed. A few minutes later, they reached the spot where they'd left KC's mom. KC stood on her tiptoes. She tried to spot her mother and the president over the other people.

"Do you see them anywhere?" she asked Marshall.

"Nope, but wait a sec." Marshall climbed onto the seat of a bench. He craned his neck, looking in all directions. "I don't see them," he said.

"That's funny," KC said. She joined Marshall on the bench. "There aren't any secret service guys, either."

"They've gotta be around here," Marshall said. "Maybe your mom and the president went for a walk."

KC shook her head. She was beginning to feel worried. "Mom wouldn't take off without letting me know," she said.

KC's ice cream cone dripped on her hand, but she ignored it. With her heart beating fast, she searched the crowd. Nowhere did she see a man in a baseball cap and a woman wearing a purple dress.

President Thornton and her mother had vanished!

2
Top Secret

"Maybe they went into one of the buildings," Marshall suggested.

KC gazed up and down the Mall. The Washington Monument was at one end, and the Capitol stood at the other. Museums lined either side of the long, grassy lawn.

KC shook her head. "Marshall, my mom has this rule—if one of us changes a plan, we tell the other one. She reminds me all the time." KC hopped off the bench and threw her unfinished cone into a trash can. "I think something happened to her and President Thornton!"

"There's something else your mom tells you all the time," Marshall said, still working on his cone. "Don't jump to conclusions."

"I'm not jumping to anything!" KC said. "She was supposed to be here, and she's not. Wouldn't you worry if your mom disappeared into thin air?"

"Okay, sure I would," Marshall agreed. "So what should we do?"

"Let's look around the Mall," KC said. "They have to be somewhere."

KC and Marshall walked the length of the Mall and back. Crowds of people were out, enjoying the sunshine and the cherry blossoms. Twenty minutes later, KC and Marshall were in front of the Air and Space Museum again.

"Something has happened to them,"

KC told Marshall. Her stomach felt jumpy, like she was about to be sick. "I think we should go home. I'm sure Mom will call me."

They retraced their steps toward home. KC studied the people around her. She kept hoping to spot that purple dress.

Back at their building, Donald held the door open for them. "Have you seen my mother?" KC asked him.

Donald looked puzzled. "Weren't you all together?"

"We were," KC explained. "But then my mom and the president disappeared. Did she come here?"

Donald shook his head. "I haven't seen her since you guys left," he said. "And I've been in the lobby the whole time."

KC had tears in her eyes. "What could

have happened to them?" she said.

Donald put a hand on her shoulder. "If Lois is with the president, I'm sure she's fine," he said. "He's always surrounded by his secret service agents."

KC nodded. "But we should go upstairs in case she calls."

"Good idea," Donald said. "I'll bet your phone rings in five minutes!" He walked with them to the elevator and took them up to the fifth floor.

KC let them in with her key. She prayed the phone would be ringing. But the apartment was silent. Lost and Found were asleep on the sofa.

KC switched on the TV and used the remote to find the local news. Standing in front of the TV, she surfed between channels. "Nothing," she muttered.

"What are you looking for?" Marshall asked. He sat next to the kittens and stroked their soft fur.

"I don't know," KC said. "But if something happened to the president, it'd be on the news, right?"

Marshall smiled at his friend. "Of course it would," he said. "So that means nothing bad has happened."

"I guess," KC said. "But Mom would never just go off somewhere!"

KC continued to surf, hitting all the news channels. Finally she gave up and punched the OFF button.

She flopped down on the floor. *Everything's going to be all right,* she told herself. But still she felt scared. And sad.

KC thought about her father down in Florida. Maybe she should call him. But she couldn't—she had to leave the phone line open.

As if by magic, the phone rang.

KC leaped up to answer it with her fingers crossed. Marshall ran into the kitchen and picked up the extension.

KC reached the phone on the second ring. "Mom?" she said.

"KC? This is the president," a familiar voice answered.

To KC, it sounded as if he had a stuffy nose. She was suspicious. The president didn't have a cold when she saw him a little while ago! "Are you with my mom?" she asked.

"No, I'm not," the president said. "That's why I called."

"Where is she?" KC almost yelled. "She was with you!"

"No, she was with Casey Marshall," the president said. "I came down with a cold, so I sent Casey to meet you instead."

"But where are they?" KC asked. "Marshall and I went to get ice cream and they disappeared!"

"KC, I'd rather talk to you about this in person," President Thornton said. "I'm sending a car to pick up you and Marshall and bring you to the White House. I'll explain everything when I see you."

"Is my mom all right?" KC asked. "Shouldn't I stay here in case she calls?"

There was silence on the phone. "I can only say I think she's fine," the president said finally. "But she isn't in a position to call you."

Now KC was really worried. Her hands felt hot and cold at the same time.

"The car will be there in five minutes," the president continued. "Will you be downstairs?"

KC gulped. "Yes, sir."

"Before you hang up," the president added, "have you told anyone else about what happened?"

"Only Donald," KC said.

There was a pause. "Okay, but please ask him not to say a word," the president warned. "This is top secret!"

3
Kidnapped

Instead of waiting for the elevator, KC and Marshall ran down the fire stairs. Donald looked surprised to see them. "Did your mom call?" he asked hopefully.

"No, but the president did," KC said. "We're going to the White House. He says my mom is all right. And he said, 'Tell Donald not to say a word to anyone!' "

Donald's face turned pink. "The president knows my name?"

KC nodded. "He wanted me to tell you it's top secret!"

"Please let the president know that these lips are sealed!" Donald closed an invisible zipper over his mouth.

"I think the car's here," Marshall said, pointing through the glass door.

"Oh my," Donald said.

The car was long and black. A small American flag flew from the antenna.

KC and Marshall hurried to the car just as the driver stepped out. Wearing a suit and tie, he walked smartly around the car and opened the rear door. "I'm here to take KC and Marshall to the White House. Is that you?"

KC looked at the man. He was tall with very short hair. His eyes were hidden behind dark glasses. KC suddenly felt wary. *Is this guy really from the White House?* she wondered. She wasn't sure she wanted to get into the car.

KC decided to test him. "The president

and I have a password," she said. "So what's the password?"

The man hesitated, then shut the door. From a pocket inside his jacket, he pulled out a cell phone. He dialed a number, waited, then spoke. "The young lady wants a password, sir," the man said.

He handed the phone to KC. "It's the president," he told her.

KC put the phone to her ear. "Hi, KC," the president said. "You are wise to be cautious. I should have thought of the password idea myself. How can I assure you that I'm the president?"

KC felt a little foolish, but she asked anyway. "What were you wearing when you came to my house in February?"

The president laughed. "Good thinking, KC. I was wearing my pajamas."

KC smiled. "Thanks, sir! See you in a few minutes." She handed the cell phone to the driver.

He was grinning. "Satisfied?"

"Yes, thank you."

He opened the door again and KC and Marshall stepped inside.

The car zoomed down Constitution Avenue, then turned through the White House gates. The driver made two more turns and stopped. "The president's private entrance," he said. He came around and opened their door. "Someone will come for you in a minute."

The driver got back into the car and drove away.

Marshall nudged KC's arm. "Look," he said.

A marine marched over to them. His

uniform was crisply pressed and his black shoes sparkled. "The president is waiting for you," he said. "Will you follow me, please?"

He turned and marched away. KC and Marshall hurried to keep up. They went through a door, down a hallway with thick carpeting, and up an elevator.

Finally they came to a wide door. The marine knocked twice with his white-gloved knuckles.

"Yes," a voice said.

The marine opened the door and stepped aside so KC and Marshall could enter.

The president was sitting in a chair. He was wearing a gray sweatshirt and baggy pants. A fluffy orange cat sat in his lap.

"Thank you, sergeant," the president

said. He looked pale, and the rims of his eyes were red and puffy.

The marine saluted, stepped back, and closed the door.

"Hi, you two," the president said. His voice was hoarse. "Come on in." Then he sneezed.

A tall woman came into the room. "Hello, I'm Vice President Mary Kincaid," she said. "Won't you have a seat?"

KC and Marshall shook her hand, then sat on a sofa.

"President Thornton hasn't much of a voice right now," the vice president said. "So I'll tell you what we know. At ten forty-two this morning, the president's secret service men reported that someone had kidnapped President Thornton."

"Obviously, they were wrong," the

president said. "For security reasons, the secret service agents hadn't been told that I sent Casey Marshall to meet you."

"Unfortunately, they took KC's mother along with Casey," Mary Kincaid said.

KC swallowed the lump in her throat. "Does anyone know where they are?"

Mary Kincaid shook her head. "No, but we've received a ransom letter by fax. The message assures us that Casey and your mother are safe and well. The kidnappers promise to let them go as soon as the White House meets their demands."

The room was silent, except for the cat's purring.

"What do they want?" Marshall asked.

"What they asked for," the president said, "is the International Space Station."

4
The Search Begins

The vice president went on. "They want to go aboard the space station," she stated. "They want to take it over."

"But aren't there astronauts living on it now?" Marshall asked.

The president nodded. "Yes, ours as well as astronauts from other countries."

"So what happens to them if the kidnappers get onboard?" KC asked.

"Everyone will have to leave," the vice president said. "Apparently, the kidnappers want to be the only folks up there."

"What are they gonna do with a space station?" Marshall asked.

"That is the question, isn't it?" the president said. "But more importantly, I want you to know, KC, that we're doing everything we can to get your mother back."

"The FBI and others are searching this town," Mary Kincaid informed the kids. "Every street has a roadblock. Every building is being searched. The bus and train stations and airport are being checked. SWAT team helicopters are in the air right now. We'll find your mother."

KC swallowed back her tears. "Thank you," she said.

"Please be my guest in the White House while we wait this out," the president offered. "You too, Marshall."

"Thank you, sir," KC said. "But is it okay if I go home and feed my cats?"

"I'll have a car take you," Mary Kincaid

said. She reached for the telephone.

"Um, we'd rather walk," KC said. "It's not far."

The president scooted the cat off his lap and stood up. "Try not to worry," he said. "We have a hundred of our best people looking for Casey and your mother. I know we'll get them back soon."

He leaned over the desk and scribbled something on a small pad. "Here's my private phone number," he said, handing the top sheet to KC. "Call if you need anything at all."

The president sneezed again. He wiped his nose with a handkerchief. "I'm going back to bed. Mary, will you show KC and Marshall the way out?"

"Of course. Come on, kids."

Mary Kincaid escorted them to the

hall, then signaled to the marine who was waiting. "Please take KC and Marshall to the special exit," she said.

"Yes, Madam Vice President," he said.

KC and Marshall followed the marine down the hall, into the elevator, and out the private exit. He gave them a salute as they headed toward Pennsylvania Avenue.

As soon as the marine was out of sight, Marshall stopped KC. "Okay, you're up to something," Marshall said. "What's this about feeding your cats? I saw you fill up their food bowl an hour ago."

"I know," KC said. "We're not going home."

"We're not? Where are we going?"

"To look for my mother." KC started walking again. Marshall hurried to keep up with her.

"But the president told us a hundred guys are already looking," Marshall said.

"And women, too, Marshall," KC said. "Not all FBI agents are men, you know."

"Okay, sue me," Marshall said. "But how are we supposed to find your mom and Casey?"

They were approaching the Museum of Natural History. Across Madison Drive, they could see the flags flying over the Smithsonian castle.

"By looking for clues," KC said.

"How can two kids . . ." Marshall stopped and gave KC a long look. KC didn't meet his eyes. "Okay," he said after a minute. "We'll do whatever you want. Where should we start?"

They ended up on Constitution Avenue, near the Washington Monument.

"Let's start here," KC said. "Then we can walk toward the Capitol. And check every building—inside and out!"

"There are a lot of buildings," Marshall said.

"So we'll split up," KC said. "We'll meet in about half an hour in front of the Air and Space Museum."

They decided that Marshall would take the buildings on the north side of the Mall. KC would check the south side. She started in the Washington Monument. From there she went to a couple of art museums, then the Smithsonian castle.

KC worked her way along the Mall, looking everywhere she could think of. She searched the sculpture gardens and the carousel. She went in every museum. Luckily, they all had free admission.

KC was hot, tired, and sweaty when she finally met Marshall by the Air and Space Museum. "Any luck?" she asked.

"No," he said. "But in the Natural History Museum, I saw a tarantula even bigger than Spike!"

KC sat down on the steps outside the space museum. "Do you want to do this one, or should I?"

"Do you really think we'll find them?" Marshall commented. "I mean—"

"We can't just go back to the White House and do nothing, Marsh," KC said. "Someone took my mom and I'm getting her back ... even if I have to search every inch of Washington, D.C.!"

5
Space Mission

"Okay, okay, we'll check in here," said Marshall. He shoved open the door of the museum. KC and Marshall were greeted by cool air and a crowd of people.

The room they entered was cavernous. The walls were glass, letting in the sunlight. Airplanes, spacecraft, missiles, rockets, and other things were on display. The Wright brothers' 1903 Flyer was there, along with the Spirit of St. Louis. Some displays were roped off to keep visitors from touching anything.

"Okay," KC said, "let's ask people if they saw the president."

They split up. KC approached a man with two little boys. They were looking at an exhibit about hot air balloons.

"Excuse me," KC said. "But have you seen the president today?"

"What president?" the man asked.

"Of the United States," KC said. "President Thornton."

"Cool!" one of the boys said. "The president is here!"

The man looked at KC. "Is he really?"

KC sighed. "I don't know," she said. "Did you see him? He was with a woman in a purple dress."

The man shook his head. "Sorry, I was too busy watching my kids."

KC asked other people. She saw Marshall doing the same thing. Everyone shook their heads, no.

She walked across the room to join Marshall. "No luck, huh?" she asked.

"Nope. But I talked to one guy who shook his hand outside."

"That was before they disappeared." KC glanced at a wide set of stairs. A small sign posted by the steps read:

More Displays on Second Floor

"Come on," she said, starting up the staircase. At the top, she stopped to watch the crowd in the main gallery.

Marshall bumped shoulders with KC. "Let's keep looking," he said.

They checked out the second floor displays. They saw war planes and an exhibit about exploring the planets. Marshall stopped in front of a meteorite found in Antarctica.

They came to an open doorway with a sign on a pedestal that read:

CAUTION—WET FLOOR
APOLLO 11
LUNAR MODULE
EXHIBIT CLOSED TODAY

A red velvet rope blocked the entrance. A man in a gray uniform was standing on the shiny floor just inside the room.

"This is so neat," Marshall said. He leaned over the rope for a better look.

In the center of the room stood the lunar module of Apollo 11, the first spacecraft to land on the moon. Under Apollo 11, a circle of dust and rocks represented the moon's surface. Twenty feet above, two fake astronauts wearing space suits

hung from cables attached to the ceiling.

"Excuse me," the man said. He was tall and thin, with a deep voice. "This exhibit is closed today."

"Sorry," Marshall said.

For about the hundredth time, KC asked, "Have you seen the president in here today? He was with my mother. She was wearing a purple dress."

The man frowned and shook his head. "I'm too busy to notice who comes in and out," he said. He left them at the door and walked toward the module.

Near the Apollo 11, the man stooped and picked something off the floor. He stared at it, glanced back at KC and Marshall, then quickly shoved it in his pocket.

"Did you see that?" KC whispered.

"What?" asked Marshall.

"There was a cherry blossom on the floor," KC said. "That janitor put it in his pocket."

Marshall shrugged. "So? There are about a million cherry blossoms all over Washington."

"But this floor has just been cleaned. No one is allowed to walk on it. So how did a cherry blossom get there?"

KC stared at the man in the gray uniform. "And besides, my mother had one in her hair," she said.

6

Flowers on the Moon

"What are you saying?" Marshall asked.

"Marsh, my mom had a pink flower in her hair when she disappeared. And there was a cherry blossom on the floor where there shouldn't be one. It doesn't make sense."

"So maybe somebody dropped it," Marshall said.

"Yes, and maybe that somebody was my mother!" KC said. "It's the first clue we've found, Marsh. Come on, let's search the rest of this place. Maybe my mother is here!"

They walked from exhibit to exhibit.

They looked in every room on the second floor, but didn't discover anything new. Marshall flopped down on a bench. KC joined him. They didn't talk.

KC sat and stared at the floor. Suddenly two pairs of feet stepped into her line of sight.

"Did you find your mother?" a familiar voice asked.

KC looked up. The feet belonged to the tall janitor they had spoken to before. Another man was with him, dressed in a similar uniform. The second janitor was short and round, with little eyes that kept blinking.

A tingly feeling crept up KC's spine. Something was wrong here. She took a deep breath and smiled at the two men. "No, but my mom is supposed to meet me here later," she said. "We're gonna hang out until then."

"Okay," the taller man said. "Just stay off the wet floor."

"Sure thing," KC said. As the men walked away, she grabbed Marshall's arm.

"What do you mean your mom's supposed to meet us here?" Marshall hissed. "What's going on?"

"Did you see the shoes those guys are wearing?" KC asked.

Marshall started to turn around.

"No, don't look now!" KC said, grabbing him again.

"How can I see their shoes if you won't let me look?" Marshall asked.

"They're wearing dress-up shoes," KC said.

Marshall stared at KC. "What do you

mean, 'dress-up' shoes? I don't get it."

"Marsh, if you were mopping floors, would you wear expensive shoes?" KC asked. "The janitor at school wears work boots or old sneakers. But those two guys are wearing good shoes, real shiny."

"And that means . . . ?"

"It means maybe they're pretending to be janitors, Marsh."

"Why would anyone pretend to be a janitor?" Marshall asked.

"That's what we need to find out," KC said. "Come on."

KC checked over her shoulder to make sure they weren't being watched. Then she led Marshall back to the Apollo 11 display.

They stopped at the red rope. KC bent down and touched the floor. "The janitor just said it was wet. But it's dry," she mumbled. "So why is the exhibit still closed?"

KC and Marshall gazed past the velvet rope. Nothing had changed. The Apollo 11 stood in the middle of the room with its spindly legs stuck in powdery "moon dust." The two fake astronauts hung from above.

Suddenly Marshall jumped. "Huh?" he said. He blinked his eyes and stared at the hanging space suits. "Did you see that?"

"See what?" KC asked.

"You're not gonna believe this," said Marshall, "but I swear one of those space suit guys just moved."

KC looked up at the hanging space suits. "Stop joking around, Marshall," she said. "They're fake." Feeling an itch, she rubbed her nose.

When she looked up again, one of the astronauts was rubbing its face mask.

"There it is again!" Marshall said. "It moved!"

"I saw it!" KC shouted. She wiggled her fingers.

The astronaut wiggled its fingers.

KC knocked the velvet rope out of the way. She sprinted into the room and waved her arms frantically at the two space suits.

Slowly, one of them waved back at her.

7
Run and Hide

"Mom!" KC screamed up at the two space suits.

"Is it them?" Marshall asked from behind KC.

"It has to be!" KC said to Marshall. "Help me figure out a way to get them down!"

"Hey, you kids! Get away from that exhibit!" a voice rang out.

"Uh-oh," Marshall muttered.

The tall janitor entered the room. "What do you think you're doing?" he asked.

The man walked slowly toward KC and

Marshall. His eyes were squinty, and his long hands curled into fists.

KC took a deep breath. Then she bent over and picked up a small rock from the pile beneath the Apollo 11.

"Thank goodness you're here!" she said, holding out the rock. "Look, I've found a clue about the missing president!"

The man's frown turned to a look of puzzlement. He stared first at the rock in KC's hand, then turned his eyes upward toward the two space suits.

Which is exactly what KC hoped he would do.

"Run!" she screamed at Marshall.

The man reached for KC, but she dodged away. He positioned himself in front of the exit with an evil sneer on his face.

Marshall charged right for the man, as if

he was going to knock him over. But at the last second, Marshall flung himself down like a kid sliding into second base. He slid across the floor, slipping right between the man's long legs. When the man whirled around, KC darted past him.

KC and Marshall dashed down the stairs and out into the crowded main room.

"This way!" KC said, running over to a group of kids. She and Marshall wiggled to the front, right next to one of the chaperones.

Safe for now, KC caught her breath. She was still holding the rock, so she slipped it into her pocket. Cautiously, she looked over her shoulder.

The man glared back at her. His face was red and his eyes flashed with anger.

She saw him start walking toward the school group.

KC forced herself to stay calm and think. He wouldn't dare grab two kids in front of all these people, would he?

She decided he would. He'd just say that these children had stolen a moon rock from the Apollo exhibit. Then he'd take her and Marshall away and . . .

KC felt herself begin to panic. The man was coming closer. Should she yell out that this guy had kidnapped the president and hidden him in a space suit?

KC realized that nobody would believe her. They'd laugh or think she was lying to get out of trouble.

Marshall tugged on her arm. "KC, that guy's getting closer! What are we gonna do?"

KC made a decision. "We have to split up," she whispered, slipping Marshall the phone number. "You call the president. Tell him we found my mom and Casey. I'll try to get that guy to follow me."

Marshall hesitated. "Okay. Be careful, KC."

"I will," KC said. "Tell the president to send the SWAT team!" Then KC turned to the group's chaperone.

"Excuse me!" she said loudly. Out of the corner of her eye, KC saw the janitor stop and watch her. "Would you please take me to the bathroom?" she asked the chaperone.

The woman looked puzzled. "You're not part of my group, are you?" she asked.

"I know," KC said. "I lost my group, and I really have to go!"

"Of course I'll take you," the chaperone said. "It's this way." She took KC's hand and they headed away from the group.

KC glanced over her shoulder. Yes! The man was following her, not Marshall. She shuddered. He reminded her of a lion stalking its prey.

The chaperone paused in front of the bathrooms. Before KC could thank her and dash inside, the man put his hand on her shoulder.

"I'm sorry," he said to the chaperone. "This girl stole something from the Apollo exhibit." He held out his large hand. "May I have it, please?"

KC gulped and looked down. The rock she had picked up made a bulge in her pocket. She slowly took it out and gave it to the man.

The kind chaperone was staring at her. KC felt her face turn red.

"Now, if you'll come with me," the man said, "I'm taking you to security."

"Is that necessary?" the chaperone asked, smiling at the fake janitor. "She's returned the rock."

The man glared at the woman. "Stealing moon rocks is a federal offense!" he said. He put his hand on KC's shoulder and led her away.

"Where are you taking me?" KC demanded.

"Quiet," the man said. His hand felt as if it were burning KC's shoulder.

They came to the Apollo exhibit. The wet floor sign was gone, and the door was closed. The man pulled a key from his pocket and inserted it into the lock. He shoved KC into the room and closed the door behind them.

The other janitor stood there with his hands on his hips and a smirk on his face. His piggy eyes blinked rapidly. When he moved aside, KC almost fainted.

Marshall was sitting on the floor beneath the Apollo. His hands and feet were bound, and a red cloth was tied around his mouth.

8
Doomed

KC felt sick. Marshall stared back at her, mumbling something through his gag.

The tall man laughed. "Waldo here caught your little friend trying to make a phone call," he said.

He held up the slip of paper with the president's phone number. He ripped it into pieces and let them fall from his hands.

KC watched the bits of paper flutter to the floor by her feet. Calling the president had been their only chance. Now no one knew where they were. She and her mom, Marshall and Casey were doomed.

With tears in her eyes, KC looked up at the two space suits. One of them waved down at her.

"Very clever of you to have found them," the tall janitor said. "What tipped you off?"

KC wiped her nose with her sleeve. "The flower you picked up," KC told the man. "My mother dropped it there."

"Well," the man said, "like Hansel and Gretel's bread crumbs, the flower won't do your mother and the president any good."

"I hope you go to jail for a million years!" KC shouted.

The man snorted. "First they have to catch me. And where I'm going, they won't."

"Please let my mother down," KC

pleaded. "She gets dizzy from heights."

"What're we gonna do with them, Chip?" Waldo asked, ignoring KC. "We don't need four hostages."

Chip laughed. "We'll take them with us," he said. "With the president as our guest, nobody will bother us. I doubt anyone will try to destroy the space station with the President of the United States aboard!"

He glanced down at the kids. "But I have other plans for the woman and these two. Once we get to the space station, they'll be taking a space walk of their own. Only they won't be wearing space suits!"

The two men high-fived each other.

"You'll never get away with this!" KC said.

"Wrong," Chip said, holding up his cell

phone. "We've just been notified that we're cleared to get on the shuttle. Ralphy's on his way with the helicopter."

"Prepare to say bye-bye to Earth," Waldo said. He pulled a rope from his pocket and began tying KC's hands behind her back.

Suddenly he stopped and looked up. His tiny eyes blinked. "Did you hear that?" he asked Chip. "I think it's our ride."

The taller man smiled. "Yes, it's the chopper. Next stop, Florida."

Waldo finished tying up KC, then sat her next to Marshall. He and Chip walked away and stood by the closed door.

KC moved closer to Marshall, directly under her mother. "I'm sorry," she whispered. She thought about her father again, and her kittens. She wondered if Marshall was thinking about his family.

Suddenly three things happened at once—a terrific crashing noise made KC jump, the door burst open, and two men thundered into the room. They were followed by about ten men and women wearing SWAT team uniforms.

One of the women strode up to Chip and Waldo, who were cringing in a corner. "Hands out and mouths shut," she said. She snapped her fingers at one of her team members. "Wrap these two to go."

"With pleasure," the man said as he clicked handcuffs onto the kidnappers' wrists.

The woman strode over and knelt in front of KC and Marshall. "Are you okay?" she asked.

KC couldn't find her voice. She nodded instead.

"Are you Marshall?" the woman asked, untying his gag.

Marshall licked his lips, then grinned and said, "Yeah. What took you so long?"

"Long?" The woman looked at her watch. "You called only ten minutes ago."

KC stared at Marshall. "You called the president's number?"

"Yup. That goon grabbed me right after I hung up." Marshall grinned. "I let him think he got me before I made the phone call."

"Marshall Li, I'm mad at you!" KC said. "Why didn't you tell me you made the call?"

Marshall held up the red cloth. "I was gagged, remember?"

9

1600 Pennsylvania Avenue

The next morning, another black car picked up KC, her mom, and Marshall. They were driven to the White House and escorted to President Thornton's private residence. They found him sipping a glass of orange juice.

"Good morning," the president said when they entered. He looked much better. His eyes were still a little red, but he wasn't sneezing anymore.

"How are you feeling?" KC asked.

"Much improved, now that I know you're all safe."

"So where's Casey?" Marshall asked.

"Poor guy, I sent him on a vacation. He's in disguise, so no one will mistake him for me this time." President Thornton looked at KC's mom. "Ms. Corcoran, please accept my—"

KC's mom interrupted. "Please call me Lois, Mr. President."

The president smiled. "Okay, if you'll call me Zach." He cleared his throat and started again. "Lois, I'm so sorry I didn't come to meet you yesterday."

Lois nodded. "At first I thought Casey was joking," she said. "He asked the secret service men to give us a moment alone and started to explain. That's when those two men grabbed us."

"Who were they, anyway?" KC asked.

The president took a sip of juice. "Chip Hornbeck and Waldo Weeks are disgruntled astronauts," he said. "They were kicked out of NASA two years ago, and never got to go into space. They were unhappy and decided to get revenge."

"So they were only pretending to be janitors, right?" KC asked.

The president nodded. "Because they were astronauts, they knew all the off-limit places in the Air and Space Museum."

Just then Marshall's stomach growled.

"Well, I guess we'd better eat," said the president. "Please sit down, everyone."

They all sat and began passing platters of scrambled eggs, fruit, and bagels. The president's cat sat by his feet and meowed loudly.

"Sorry, George," the president said. He dropped a cherry onto the carpet.

"Why did you name him George?" Marshall asked.

The president grinned. "For the first president," he said. "And you know how he liked cherries!"

George held the cherry with his front paws and took delicate bites.

"Anyway," the president continued, "Chip and Waldo will be in jail for quite a long time."

"There was a third man," KC's mom said. "He was waiting inside the rear door of the museum. He had rags dipped in something awful that they put over our faces. When I woke up, they were putting me in that space suit!"

"Ralphy Bird," the president said. "We've already got him. He was caught in a helicopter, hovering over the museum."

"Was it scary hanging up there?" Marshall asked KC's mom.

"Oh, honey, you have no idea!" she said. "When I saw you two walk into the room, I thought I was dreaming."

"And we might not have gone in if KC hadn't seen the flower you dropped."

KC's mother laughed. "I shook it out of my hair when they were stuffing me into that space suit," she said. "I prayed someone would spot it there."

The president grinned. "Good thinking, Lois!" He picked up his juice glass. "Here's a toast to KC and Marshall. What would the White House do without you two?"

That night, KC and Marshall were watching TV. Lost and Found chased each other around the apartment.

A buzzer sounded. KC's mom walked over to the door and pressed a button.

"Sorry to disturb you, Ms. Corcoran," Donald's voice said from the wall unit. "I have a package for you."

"For me? Okay, send it up."

A few minutes later, she opened the door. Donald grinned and handed her a long white box.

"What is it, Mom?" KC got up and walked over to the door.

"It looks like flowers," her mother said. She removed the lid. Under a layer of tissue paper lay two dozen yellow roses.

"Oh my goodness!" KC's mom said. "Who would send me roses?"

A small envelope was taped to the box. "There's a note, Mom—read it!" KC said.

KC's mother opened the envelope and

pulled out a card. She read it silently, then began to smile.

"No fair," KC said. "Read it out loud!"

Blushing, Lois Corcoran read the card:

Dear Lois,

Please accept my apology for your terrible experience yesterday. May I make it up to you with dinner at the White House tomorrow night? This time I promise to show up!

Fondly,
Zach Thornton

Fondly? thought KC. *The president asked my mom on a date!*

Calendar Mysteries

Help Bradley, Brian, Lucy, and Nate . . .

. . . solve a mystery a month!

If you like Capital Mysteries,
you might want to read
A to Z Mysteries!

Help Dink, Josh, and Ruth Rose . . .

. . . solve mysteries from A to Z!